T0121759

Psyche and Self's Theories in Psychology.

A concise comparison of a number of theorists like Carl Jung and Abraham Maslow's general concepts of the self and the psyche.

This book attempts to find a common ground between Jung's general concepts of individuation, wholeness, spirituality, and religion and those of Maslow's self-actualization and homeostasis besides using other scholar's concepts to find a common ground.

This is an up to the point comparison of a number of theories for sophisticated thinkers who are looking for answers for their spiritual sides.

By: Roya R. Rad, MA, PsyD

Note to the reader: Throughout this book, the subjects he as well as she are both referred to as she. This is in no way a matter of preference but of simplicity. In addition, the character of this book, Marry, sometime uses direct quotes from sources which can be found through the reference section

Disclaimer

The publisher and the author make an effort to give valid information to the public;
however, they make no guarantee with respect to the accuracy or completeness of
the contents of the books published. Science is unlimited, and there are many facts
yet to be discovered and improved upon, as the world expands. The information
that SKBF Publishing presents to the public can only be used as a personal
enhancing device for building a healthy lifestyle. The reader is always responsible for
using the information the best possible way, according to his or her unique needs,
environment, and personality. Books, lectures, websites and other forms of self-help
tools are general and valuable tools for a person looking for self-education, but
sometimes they are more like statistical information. They will give us a general idea
about most people, but we have to remember that each of us is a unique individual,
and treatment for our healing process would have to be administered accordingly.

Printed in Victoria, BC, Canada.

ISBN: 978-1-4269-2697-6 (sc)

*Our mission is to efficiently provide the world's finest, most comprehensive book
publishing service, enabling every author to experience success. To find out how to
publish your book, your way, and have it available worldwide, visit us online at
www.trafford.com*

Trafford rev. 2/2/2010
Co Published in USA by SKBF Publishing www.SKBFPublishing.com
Edited by: Walter L. Kleine, Kleine Editorial Services

 www.trafford.com
North America & international
toll-free: 1 888 232 4444 (USA & Canada)
phone: 250 383 6864 ♦ fax: 812 355 4082

Contents

An Overview

It seems like some psychologists, including analytical ones, may be misrepresenting Jung's views when it comes to the application of his theories and his theories of survival. Jung seems to have combined a biological and a social perspective of the psyche, where he looked at the psyche's inherent social aspects. He is interested in the thought process of people like Burckhardt.

Jung is becoming more of an interest to modern society and those thinkers who would like to understand the psyche for spiritual reasons, and from a logical, and in some ways scientific, point of view.

Jung was one of Freud's students, but moved away from him during the course of his professional career, though he maintained his respect for Freud. In one of his analyses of the difference between himself and Freud, he says, "My attitude to biology is equally positive, and to the empiricism of natural science in general, in which I see a Herculean attempt to understand the psyche by approaching it from the outside world, just as religious gnosis is a prodigious attempt of the human mind to derive knowledge of the cosmos from within. In my picture of the world, there is a vast outer realm and an equally vast inner realm; between these two stands man, facing now one and now the other, and according to temperament and disposition, taking the one for the absolute myth by denying or sacrificing the other."

In Jung's views and theory it is apparent that he wants to understand the psyche from a more multifaceted dimension, and is not satisfied with aggression and sex being the roots of every human's motivation. He continuously questions the unconscious, and says that the unconscious is not a specific thing, but rather something unknown which affects us in every moment.

Jung views an individual in terms of a whole combined of opposite parts. The more a person becomes her whole self, the more she is able to comprehend and accept her every element. The more she does that, the more liberated she feels; an inner liberation that is reflected and projected into the external world. This acceptance includes the person's persona (what we show the world) and shadow (the undiscovered aspect of us, which we repress and deny the existence of).

To describe shadow a little more, Jung identifies the word shadow as an individual's negative and repressed parts, which they project onto others. This could be anything from repressed unresolved issues, or out of balance feelings like fear, anger, jealousy, resentment, hate, etc. Therefore, the individual's unreasonable rejection of others is ultimately an unconscious rejection of parts of themselves. For example, when we hate something in someone, it would be helpful to self-reflect and see what the root of that is. Maybe, just maybe, it is a repressed trait of our own being that needs our attention. While having a preference and being attracted to certain elements are natural parts of being a human, having strong negative feelings toward someone without a solid reason could be a projection of the shadow, which we need to look into. Further, shadow is an essential part of the process of individuation, because it helps with the mechanism of self-understanding and differentiation.

When it comes to the process of differentiation, humans have to first set apart from their source to be able to find their individuality within the source. After that, they can connect back to the source with a sense of self-knowledge. In other words, after going through the individuation process, one can function from wholeness, but with full awareness and knowledge of the parts. Knowing the shadow is an important part of this individuation process.

Until we acknowledge the shadow's existence, it controls us. It is only when we understand and are willing to admit that we, like anyone else, have shadows that we can learn to deal with it and be in control of it. For example, consider a person who has some form of inner anger. If such a person is not aware of this part of her shadow, she may act excessively calm to give the persona of not being angry. In the meantime, just because she is denying this anger does not mean that it does not exist in her. On the other hand, it exists and is in full power and control over her because she is unaware of it. Such a person may not actively act angry by yelling or shouting, but will passively bring out this part of the shadow without being aware of it. This could be her being jealous of others, hurtful sarcasm, feeling anger at the wrong source, acting discriminatory toward others, gossiping about others, wanting to step over others to achieve goals, feeling happy for other people's misery, taking advantage of others, or an inability to feel other people's pain, etc. If we think that we don't have any of these characteristics, it would be good to think again! Sometimes, an authentic self-discovery brings out surprises. Self-reflection is the key to releasing any negative inner feelings and thoughts that result in negative behaviors, it is the key to self realization.

For Jung, the process of self-realization is not walking toward perfection but getting one step closer to the individual's wholeness; the sum of her parts. The process of moving toward this wholeness is different for different individuals and cannot be imitated. Jung did not encourage following someone else, but learning from others and choosing one's own path. When discovering a sense of wholeness, perfection is self-limiting because if we look for perfection, we are putting an end to an endless process of self-discovery. This can lead us to stepping into something with unreasonable expectations, creating disappointments. Self-discovery is like an onion; peel one layer and there comes another, and there is no ending point, but a process.

Life is a route we take to become aware of our wholeness through interaction, reflection, learning, and growing. To have a full experience, one may need to feel some form of discomfort at times because life is not about avoiding what does not feel comfortable. To experience life fully, one has to realize that it is a combination of opposites. For anything to come into existence, there has to exist an opposite to make it noticeable. For example, if we want to feel happy with our life, we have to take steps for that happiness. Those steps will probably bring about some challenges that may impose experiences of discomfort or even pain. The question is whether the pain is worth the gain? Does the benefit outweigh the cost? Is the gain a real gain that adds to the content of our life, or is it just some impulsive desire? If the first, how much would we be willing to pay for it? It all goes back to the cost and benefit analysis and applying this analysis can help in achieving a state of inner balance.

When it comes to self-realization, Maslow is another well known psychologist who addresses this concept in great detail. He came up with the term self-psychology, and described a pyramid of self-growth. I have talked about Maslow's pyramid of growth in my other books, and will touch on it briefly here. What many people, including some psychologists, do not notice is the similarities that exist between Jung and Maslow's foundations and concepts related to self psychology. They may use words differently, but there seems to be many of the same underlying explanations and at points, t complement each other. For example, Jung's term, shadow, seems analogous to Maslow's term, evil. Maslow's self-actualization seems similar to Jung's self-realization, and Maslow's self-transformation seems similar to Jung's definition of wholeness.

Maslow says that evil is people's own ignorance when they neglect their potential; the unused and wasted power that decays and brings disease. What one does not grow within might turn against one. In the same way, Jung explains that the shadow is the repressed part that is creating negativity.

Maslow and Jung explain the process of self-discovery

in terms of self-actualization and self-realization. To describe self-actualization, one needs to be familiar with Maslow's pyramid of growth, which has about seven levels, starting with the basic needs, and going up to the higher needs. Maslow says that in order for an individual to get to the process of self-actualization, which is a need on top of his pyramid, she should satisfy and pay attention to her lower needs first. The lower needs start with basic physiological needs, like food, to a sense of physical security, to the ability to have secure relationships, to needs for esteem, and all the way to outer and inner self-value, self-actualization, and self-transformation. Maslow does say that an individual could go back and forth with satisfying these needs, but the higher up the pyramid, the more in control and aware the person becomes of how and when she wants to satisfy these needs. In other words, the person is in charge of when to satisfy a need, rather than the need being the driving force. In addition, there have been cases in which an individual has been able to compensate for an unmet need through other healthy means, therefore releasing the inner force created by the unmet need. Therefore, with Maslow's pyramid, depending on individual's unique personality and how one moves up, one can compromise fulfilling a need by replacing it with something else, or can go back and forth between needs.

When it comes to self actualization, we all innately have the need to self-actualize, but most of us forget to go there, not because we are incapable, but because we get preoccupied with satisfying the lower needs and never look up to see that there is something higher we can reach. Somewhere down the pyramid, we start walking in circles rather than moving up to the top of Maslow's pyramid which is self actualization.

Self-actualized people have peak experiences, look at the world from a more expanded perspective, are authentic, have an innate thirst for knowledge, are unique, have a sense of ecstasy and wonder for life, function based on their core state of being rather than an outsider's expectations, and have confidence in the world and their life.

In addition, self-actualized people have a great sense of autonomy and independence, are well aware of the surrounding culture and their environment, and have a deep understanding of them, but are not limited by their conditioning. Self-actualized people are not as dependent on the outer world for their sense of inner satisfaction as other people may be, their sense of satisfaction is not extrinsic. They are determined and motivated by signals and clues which are mostly internal rather than social, and at the same they are logical individuals and use their reason when making decisions. Self-development and inner growth are the number one priority of a self-actualized human being.

For Jung, self development is an essential part of life. He encourages individuals to go through the process of self-development and growth, and to be their own guide with knowledge and understanding, not to live through ignorance, and not to be blind followers of the outside world.

There are similarities between Jung and Maslow's explanation of self-actualized humans. In addition, these concepts seem similar to the experiences of some of the mystics, and to Assagioli's concepts of the higher self.

More specifically, Jung's concept of the self, wholeness, full potential, and the unifying law behind psychological aspects all seem to be parallel to Maslow's self-actualization and self-transformation concepts.

Roberto Assagioli was a psychiatrists who developed the concept of psychosynthesis. He states that self awareness is a spiritual goal of self realization and agrees with Freud that healing childhood upset and forming a healthy ego are essential to psychotherapy but does not believe that human growth is limited to these. He supports the idea of human potential and self actualization as well as transpersonal development. In addition, he recognizes the process of self realization as the person's response to a deeper calling.

According to Assagioli, an individual has to learn ways to eliminate conflicts and obstacles, both conscious and unconscious ones that block inner harmony and development of the personality, in addition to that the individual has to learn to use stimulation techniques to develop the weak and immature sides of the self.

Assagioli explains the self in terms of an egg diagram with seven areas: The lower unconscious, the middle unconscious, the higher unconscious, the field of consciousness, the conscious self or "I", the higher self, and the collective unconscious.

The lower unconscious is the part of the individual in which there is an experience of shame, fear, pain, despair, and rage related to the wounds suffered in life. The middle unconscious supports the individuals conscious functioning from walking to talking, and from language formation to mastering a skill and developing social roles. Assagioli reports that the higher unconscious is "our higher potentialities which seek to express themselves, but which we often repel and repress" and contact with the higher unconscious is experienced thought peak experience which is a term Maslow uses. This is an experience of a sense of deeper meaning to life, a sense of inner peace, a universality to the existence.

The next level which is the "I" is the direct projection and reflection of self. This is a vital part of the individual which is distinct but not separate from all other content. "I" has consciousness and will. It has the ability to influence the content of awareness and either expand or contract it. "I" is the experience, it is the subject and is a reflection of self. The next area is the self which is distinct but not separate from all other areas. This can also be called the higher or transpersonal self. It is a source of wisdom and guidance within the person.

According to Assagioli, these stages are a single process not a linear form and any of these stages can be present at any given moment throughout the process. An individual can go through the process thought knowledge of her personality, self control of different elements of the self, discovery of one's true self, and the formation of personality around a new center. Many of Assagioli's concepts are similar to that of Jung's.

Jung's terms become more mystic when he tries to expand the unconscious part of the psyche. He states that the self is not just the center of this life, but the perimeter which holds both conscious and unconscious; the center of wholeness. Maslow did not openly admit to any mystic form of existence when explaining humans, but it can be seen in the depth of his writings, specifically in his concept of self-transformation, which comes after a state of self-actualization has been achieved. In addition, Maslow's concept of peak experiences seems more mystic in nature.

These definitions and explanations are comparable to traditional mystic views that emphasize a soul or higher self, which needs to be discovered if the individual wants to get to a state of self-realization. Further, there are related concepts between Maslow and Jung in that they both seem to express the fact that self-discovery becomes possible when something lower, either the lower self or lower needs, quiets down and gives control to the higher ones. One can argue that it is, after all, the lower self that has lower needs. These scholars, who dared to go further than their time, seem to agree that self-discovery takes place when the inferior self falls silent and the superior self is in control; when there is an awareness and a state of being from a more mature and evolved form of functioning.

Both Maslow and Jung encouraged self-knowledge, and found it vital to mental health. This is common with many other psychologists, starting with Freud. Maslow says that Freud's most important discovery was that he identified the single most essential factor in mental illness to be the fear one may have of knowing herself. Knowing the self involves getting to know one's emotions, impulses, memories, capacities, potentialities, and destiny. Whether negative or positive, many of us spend a lifetime avoiding some of these.

As I said earlier, Maslow's concept of self-actualization seems to be pointing at an essential inner nature similar to a higher, more advanced and civilized self, which Jung also identifies with. These concepts are like those of other psychologists (some call them the adult self, parent self, or the guide self). Maslow and Jung both state that repressing or pushing any part of the self aside will not make it go away. On the other hand, any sort of psychological health will be jeopardized by failing to acknowledge all there is to the self.

Acceptance of self with all its elements, shadow, archetypes, impulses, emotions, memories, lower parts, higher parts, etc., is a characteristic of a well-developed self, and will ultimately help the individual in accepting herself, which will manifest itself through being more accepting toward the external world. It is what the individual accepts that she can change. If one lives in denial of the existence of something within, one is only empowering it.

People who can accept their own nature without feeling inferior can grow faster than those who deny, repress, or project these reactions. Maslow uses a specific example of this acceptance, saying that one does not complain because rocks are hard or water is wet. A healthy, developing individual will observe rather than judge, and will try to make improvements on a regular basis.

Maslow's similarities with mystical writers can be seen in other areas of his writings. For example he reports that the experience of a self-actualized person is a naturalistic process which does not depend on anything outside the relationship between individual's psychology and the world.

Jung and Maslow are among the main psychologists who brought out the concepts of transpersonal psychology. Some call Jung the first representative of a transpersonal orientation in psychology. He is one of the first psychologists who discussed the term wholeness in detail. Jung states, "The attainment of wholeness requires one to stake one's whole being. Nothing less will do; there can be no easier conditions, no substitutes, and no compromises."

Maslow contributes the term transpersonal psychology, and views the new field of humanistic psychology as incomplete. He states that even though science is an important aspect of learning about the self, too much focus on the scientifically-based territory of the mind would limit the state of being human. There has to be a balance, if there is no balance, it may be like there is no God, and things are based only on senses and empirical findings, but are not transcendent. Not long after that comment, Maslow came up with the term, transpersonal psychology.

Even though most intellectuals agree that relying on logic and factual findings are the most solid way to approach the concept of self-knowledge, at the same time there has to be a middle point between logic and internal clues. If one puts too much weight on empirical data to prove everything, she may lose some of the knowledge that can be achieved though inner signals.

Primitive vs. Advanced—
Mature vs. Immature—
Evolved vs. Narrowed Mind

Jung discusses the term "primitive society" in terms similar to that of Levy-Bruhl who was a French anthropologist. Levy Bruhl states that the primitive mind does not distinguish the supernatural from reality but uses mystical forms to manipulate the world. In addition, it does not address contradictions, speculation and logic.

When it comes to Jung, he believes that the mentality of a primitive man works differently from that of a modern man. Modern man's thought is more rational, but primitive man's thought is more pre-logical and collective, meaning not individuated. A primitive man is not in control of his emotions, and is unable to differentiate subject vs. object. For a primitive-minded man, everything is subjective and personalized. A primitive mind follows everyone else instead of himself.

Jung further states that a primitive thought is not

conscious. All the experiences of such an individual is processed and understood unconsciously rather than rationally. Something else is controlling him; something he is not aware of. Such an individual's mental condition confuses dream and reality in the most puzzling way, and he may spend a lifetime chasing something that is not real, only to feel disappointment and distress.

Jung states that a primitive mentality is far less developed in intensity and range. In that case, tasks like thinking and willpower are not distinguished and are pre-conscious. For example, a primitive mind does not think consciously, but a thinking pattern does appear while it cannot declare that it is thinking. It is most likely that the person holding this mind experiences it as something thinking in her. This thought-spontaneous process does not lie in her conscious, but in her unconscious. Therefore, the level of awareness is low.

Primitive mind has no distinction between the products of visions and those of the sensory experience. Psychotherapists see it in patients as how mythical fantasies happen. These fantasies are not thought through, but come out as images or chains of ideas that force their way out of the mind's unconscious. When these images are described, they have the form of mythical production. A primitive mind has no conscious wish, will, and decision, lives in the dominion of the unconscious, and is the follower of the outside world without understanding why. This is where impulsivity comes into the picture.

This seems similar to what Maslow reports when discussing individuals who live at the lower levels of the pyramid of self-growth. It seems like the primitive side is the driving force with an intention to satisfy lower needs, not thinking consciously about the higher levels of existence and needs. Maslow has a great impact on scientific views of subjects like Eastern mysticism and meditation. He seems uneasy accepting the metaphysical assumptions related to these traditions, but considers the wisdom worthy of note and learning. He points to the fact that authentic mystics, who are very rare (and usually not easy to catch), have given us insight into our deeper potentials, like altruism, compassion, aesthetics, courage, and similar characteristics.

Maslow's description of self-actualization and peak experience is similar to some of the characteristics of an authentic mystic. He states that society has a part in helping people gain self-actualization by providing the environment with educational tools. These educational tools can encourage and help people understand positive ways of thinking and living, listening to authentic inner feeling and voices, and transcending negative and unproductive environmental and cultural conditioning. Conditioning, while needed for a primitive self's survival, could be unproductive, if not destructive, for a higher self.

Religion and Spirituality

When it comes to religion and spirituality, Jung and Maslow's theories are unique in their own way, but share a common fiber, which seems to be offering an alternative to traditional religious beliefs. Jung seems to want to find an alternative to Christianity for a mind that seeks reason behind stories and rituals. He states that psychology satisfies the same needs as religion, with a more rational and up-to-date approach. Therefore, for the modern mind, psychology can be the answer.

The role that religion is seen to play is categorized into two distinct levels of individual and society. Jung discusses the positive and potentially nurturing roles that religion could play in an individual's development, if used properly. In addition, he sees religion in terms of coming out of an individual's psyche, and his concept of the collective unconscious is close in definition to that of the Eastern mystical traditions. Jung identifies the psyche as being dynamic, with different parts that relate to each other. He differentiates between conscious, unconscious, and collective unconscious.

Jung says that personality has racial or phylogenetic origins, going through the revolutionary process rooted in the individual's inheritance and memories of the past experiences of the human race. The base of personality includes archaic, primitive, innate, unconscious, and universal components. Inherited thought patterns from past generations predispose individuals to see and react to situations in the world from a conditioned way. For example, archetypes like persona, earth mother, child, wise man, and anima-animus are universal archetypes.

Personality is the psyche, and includes all thought, feeling, and behavior, whether conscious or unconscious. This psyche is the guiding force helping us adapt to our social life and environment. The psyche needs to be explored to find a state of wholeness. It corresponds to a unified whole. The purpose of life is to reach the potential of discovering wholeness and develop to the optimal level. Jung defines personality as "the supreme realization of the innate idiosyncrasy of a living being, it is an act of high courage flung in the face of life, the absolute affirmation of all that constitutes the individual, the most successful adaptation to the universal conditions of existence coupled with the greatest possible freedom for self-determination."

Personality's structure is composed of: 1. Conscious, which is where the ego operates. 2. Unconscious, which is the where the complexes and archetypes operate on a personal conscious level. 3. All levels consisting of attitudes and functions. Over time, the conscious and unconscious should blend within the individual through the self.

The conscious level of psyche includes the ego. It forms early in life, maybe even before birth. Jung warned of the danger of becoming one-sided during the process of becoming conscious, he always attempted to see both sides. The first development of the ego is the infant's discriminating process. Ego is like a door keeper, and makes determinations of which thoughts and feelings can get into consciousness. It filters experience with an attempt to maintain coherence within the personality, and give the individual a sense of identity.

According to Jung, everything we experience, including suppressed memories, will stay with us. They do not vanish. They are accumulated in the unconscious. Groups of feelings, memories, and thoughts in the personal unconscious that have strong emotional substance to them form a complex. A complex is a preoccupation with something that affects all of the individual's behavior and thought patterns. Complexes are unconscious, and everyone experiences mild forms of them and is affected by them. In the right form, they may even lead to outstanding accomplishments.

We are living to experience our archetypes and learn to connect to life. That is the way to reach our wholeness. In order to do that, we need to experience life to the fullest. If we avoid understanding an aspect of our life and do not have other ways to compromise, we lose the opportunity to learn about that aspect, and therefore block a part of us. Encountering birth, death, marriage or relationships, interactions, childhood, maturation, transformation; roles like mother, father, lover, hero, servant, and so on, are all aspects of life. The more roles we take, the more we learn through experience. The more we learn, the closer we get to our wholeness. We are always taking on some part of the archetype to feel a sense of connection with life and our surroundings. Otherwise we feel isolated and away from reality. We cannot do something just for us; we have to experience it in connection with others to get to our fullest and to give meaning to our life and our experience with it.

Going back to religious concepts, Jung does not seem to acknowledge the traditional roles of churches and their morality. He states that Christianity seems to have lost its emotional benefits for the advanced mind. This could also be applied to other religions, since religion in general seems to have failed to answer many questions that an evolved mind may have. But Jung's emphasis on Christianity is due to the fact that he was a Christian and knowledgeable about its origin, history, and rituals. He further states that as a result of this lack of emotional benefit, Westerners have lost ways to engage their archetypes and are experiencing an unbalanced psyche component. Jung attempts to define a superior or deeper being into supra-historical and trans-cultural archetypes. He states that these archetypes are present in everyone and should be engaged, and that an individual "himself is an entire church."

Maslow's identification of religion seems to consist of an illumination of a first holy figure and an experience and cultivation of the mass. Religion, according to Maslow, would be an effort of communicating peak experiences to those who have not yet experienced them. According to Maslow, religions have a basic similarity, and they should make compromises and work together to create a general belief. This universality would be a transcendent experience. Maslow believes that an important part of religion is the peak experience, which is a process of individuation. Individuation is when the person becomes what she is supposed to be, similar to what Jung would define as functioning from a whole self after knowing what it is.

Maslow explains a peak experience as a feeling of universal unity and purpose, equality and inner connectivity of all, forming the bigger picture. This experience needs an intense concentration in all areas, including visual, auditory, and tactile perception, and cannot be accomplished through a needy, egoistic, and selfish state. In addition, it can bring an optimistic outlook on life, presenting it in a more positive light.

Maslow, similar to Jung, feels that there is an evil, but that it has its own place in the world and cannot be judged or repressed but has to be acknowledged and understood. Only then can a well-developed mind deal with this "evil" and bring out the good. In other words, change comes after recognition. One can't change what one represses, she only make it denser.

Maslow believes that everyone is able to have peak experiences if she is able to overcome her fear of facing it, or is able to walk out of her comfort zone and can see that there is something deeper and higher to be discovered and accomplished. If a non-seeker does not avoid these experiences, trying to explain them in a solidly logical way, and if she learns not to think of them in a material way, she can open the door to herself and the source that lies within.

Other reasons that some people do not have peak experiences are immaturity in spiritual matters and a sense of under-appreciation for spiritual implications. Maslow states that we can learn a lesson from a true and authentic mystic, and that is that we can find sacredness in the ordinary, and in daily life and surroundings. To look far away from us for a miracle is an ignorant act, since everything around us is miraculous.

Concept of Personality and Psyche

Other scholar's concepts, like those of Wilber, are worthy of note, since they can also be related to both Jung and Maslow's concepts. Maslow's hierarchy of needs and growth, especially the one he presents toward the end of his life, in which he adds another level after self-actualization, labeled self-transformation, seems similar to Wilber's model of personality.

Wilber's model of development is more of a linear format following a straight slope from pre egoic levels to egoic ones and all the way to trans egoic levels of development. It has an arrangement of a ladder since it follows a hierarchy of psychic structure. According to this model, any psychic structure is just a potential until development occurs and makes it active. This is a complex model but explains human personality as a multi level manifestation of a single consciousness.

Wilber's spectrum of consciousness includes:

Shadow, ego, bisocial, existential, transpersonal, and mind. Shadow holds the disowned and projected aspects of the ego which seem to be external (in Jung's terms, this level holds the persona externally and the shadow internally). Ego holds filtered memories representing the total experience in a symbolic way. Bisocial represents consciousness that is above the ego oriented consciousness but not at the existential level. Existential is where consciousness is separate from its environment and is dualistic, the beginning of time and space. Transpersonal is a representation of consciousness at the transpersonal level in between existential and mind where non duality splits into duality. Mind is the highest point of absolute subjectivity, the foundation ground of all the other levels of consciousness. At mind level, consciousness is non dual.

Wilber's model attempts to blend psychology and religion or spirituality. It assumes that human psyche can be linked to electromagnetic spectrum of physics. It reports that many different schools of psychology leave out the fact that consciousness is multidimensional while focusing only on certain areas of the spectrum and ignoring the others. For example, Freudian approach is more to the shadow level but beyond that it is non effective. Wilber's model focuses on linear evolution. He reports that evolution is a transcending process helping one go beyond what went before. In other words, evolution integrates whatever was before but adds new and expanded components on a continuous base. Wilber's model of personality has no definite boundaries. He explains personality as derived from consciousness; a beam of light which is going through a prism which he calls the spectrum of consciousness. Wilber states that at the mind level, which is the deepest reality, mind becomes like an infinite and eternal ocean. During this level, man becomes one with everything else, and this is the true state of consciousness. When an individual decides to go through self-reflection, she overcomes archetypes to break through the bottom of the bucket and resolve the dualism of being subjective and objective. This is similar to the concept of self-transformation in Maslow's model.

Wilber's concepts are parallel to Jung when he discusses transpersonal bands that include archetypes. According to Wilber, a transpersonal band is a state in which man's boundaries are unlimited, but at the same time he is not aware of this freedom; in Jung's term, a state of wholeness. Wilber says that an individual can distance herself from any problems she faces (e.g anxiety or depression) and observe them objectively from outside, a whole point. This is similar to Jung's psychoanalysis.

When Jung discusses the relationship between conscious and unconscious, he says that one must bring about a bridge between the two to be able to reach a sense of wholeness. This must be done in all levels of the psyche. If one attends to the unconscious levels, one can achieve balance, creativity, and health. One has to learn to be respectful of the unconscious, and the center's guidance, intuitions, feelings, and values. The ego does play a part in this process, and is needed to uphold a logical sense of self that is not conquered by an unrestrained outpouring of the unconscious filling. This has a particular function; it helps one to choose what is to be attended to while making a decision as to how to act or react. Therefore, the conscious and unconscious parts of the psyche have an essential relationship with each other. One can use an active imagination to enable a sort of inner dialog between the two.

When Jung was working with the unconscious material, this technique, called active imagination, came about, creating a relationship with different aspects of the unconscious. This active imagination has been described differently by different people. For example, Davidson says that the transference is a form of an imaginary dialog between the part of the individual which he labels as the ego, and another form that appears to be the analyst and comes for the most part from the inner world, or the unconscious. Sometimes this dialog takes place within the individual; at other times it is a shared process of active imagination.

With Jung's active imagination, one can find an active role in communicating with the unconscious material within the psyche. This is different than simple daydreaming, because it encourages the participant to be active in the process, rather than just observing. Jung's developmental model is more of a spiral shape rather than linear. It is a dynamic model in which the self is at the center of the psyche looking externally at the conscious ego. The conscious ego interacts with the physical world using persona. As reported earlier, Assagioli has something similar but he divides the unconscious into three levels (lower, middle and higher).

In Jung's model, the psychic energy called libido flows between all areas of the psyche. The ego is to develop and mature during the first half of life and it is supposed to individuate itself from the unconscious self. During the second half of life, the ego incorporates the self by becoming aware of it. This incorporation, if done right, can give the ego a sense of meaning and fulfillment in life. The psyche and the ego are supposed to function together in a symbiotic relationship to bring about a healthy growth.

Jung's model is a spiral one because at the end the ego returns back to the self. The first half of life is focused on environmental and cultural processes, gaining skills, raising a family, self discipline, while the second half is supposed to be focused on achieving a sense of wholeness.

Related to the structure of consciousness in the evolutionary process and its development, there is an ego, which is the center of the conscious personality since the individual is born. Jung says that this ego is less developed in some cultures, but that at the end it will be an individual choice as to how much it can grow. The other category is the personal unconscious, which is the environment in which the consciousness emerges from.

The human psyche consists of the personal unconscious as well as the collective unconscious and the archetypes. The unconscious is under the conscious area, and is the place from which the consciousness emerges. Right below the conscious is the personal unconscious, which is where person's character is established. It is also where personal experiences are placed, and complexes lie within this personal consciousness. Complexes are results of traumatic experiences or incompatible tendencies. Some of these complexes and unresolved problems are essential for psychic activity.

Even deeper than the personal unconscious is another

part called the collective unconscious. This was identified by Jung through work with his patients and their dreams and fantasies. These dreams and fantasies had origins that could not be traced to the personal experiences of the individuals. Since these ideas were similar to religious and mythical themes, Jung referred to them as primordial images or archetypes.

Jung believes that archetypes are "forms without content," not past memories. These archetypes represent specific perception and action. Archetypes are "the ruling powers, the gods, images of the dominant laws and principles, and of typical, regularly occurring events in the soul's cycle of experience." Archetypes influence the human aspects of the human world and its experience. According to Jung, there are many archetypes, but a complete explanation of them is not possible.

Jung's research of religions and mythologies, in addition to his psychiatric work, helped him identify different types of archetypes. These include the persona, shadow, anima/animus, mother, child, wise old man, and self.

The persona, which is a mask people wear to hide their true nature, is a compromise between a person's real individuality and society's expectations. Professional titles, roles, and habits of social behavior are some examples of persona. Persona brings a form of social order as well as protects individual's privacy, but when the ego identifies with the persona and confuses it with the real self, the person becomes vulnerable to the unconscious.

Another of Jung's terms, shadow, can help the person get closer to self-realization, if an individual recognizes it. This is the negative, or more primitive, side of the personality. It is what we deny having, including animal tendencies inherited from our infra-human ancestors. This shadow corresponds to the personal unconscious. The more unaware of the shadow we are, the blacker and denser it is and the more control it has. The more dissociated it is from our conscious life, the more it will display a compensatory demonic dynamism. It is often projected outwards on individuals or groups, who are then thought to embody all the immature, evil, or repressed elements of the individual's own psyche (symbols of the devil and the serpent contain elements of the shadow).

Anima-Animus is one of Jung's archetypes, which follows a person's coming to terms with her shadow. After that, she is confronted with the problem of the anima/animus, the archetype which is said to personify the soul, or inner attitude. It is usually a persona that takes on the characteristics of the opposite sex. The anima is said to represent the feminine in men, and comes from three sources: 1. The individual man's experience with women as companions. 2. Man's own femininity—rooted presumably in the minority of female genes and hormones present in a man's body. 3. The inherited collective image that has been formed from man's collective experience of woman throughout the centuries.

Anima often appears in dreams, as long as she remains unconscious. She may also be projected outwards onto various women—first the mother, then lover and wife, as one grows. This projection is said to be responsible for the passionate attraction or aversion, and a man's general apprehension of the nature of women. If a man mistakenly identifies with the anima, Jung says, she can produce effeminacy or homosexuality. The anima remains in a compensatory relationship with the outer, conscious attitude. The more a man identifies with the masculine persona, the more he will be subject to the projections of his anima.

After the middle of life, the anima is essential for vitality, flexibility and human kindness. She appears in a variety of manifestations which reflect her bipolarity. If he is unconscious of her, she can be both positive and negative from one moment to another, young and then old, mother and then lover, good and then evil, and so on. She can be an ambivalent image, has occult connections with the ancient mysteries, and hence has a religious tinge.

The animus is the comparable counterpart in the female psyche. (Naomi Goldenberg's critique points out that Jung provides empirical evidence for anima, but the animus is just a postulate opposite). Animus is said to be the woman's image of a man. Unlike the anima, the animus appears in a plurality of forms. To Jung, this reflects the differences in male and female conscious attitudes. He says that the woman's consciousness tends to be exclusively personal and centered upon the family, while the man's is made up of various worlds, of which the family is only one. Thus, he finds the anima and animus to be the opposites of these conscious attitudes, plural and singular respectively.

For the anima, Eros is the undifferentiated unconscious principle (the root of all emotions), for the animus it is logos (the woman's mind responsible for unreasoned opinion and critical argumentativeness). Emma Jung, Jung's wife and a prominent psychiatrist, reports that animus manifests itself most often in words and not images, typically as a voice that comments on a person's situation or imparts general rules. When it does take a form, usually in dreams, it appears as a "plurality of men, a group of fathers, a council, a court, or some gathering of wise men, etc." It may also manifest itself in the single figure of a real man—father, lover, brother, teacher, judge, sage, etc. It is, in short, a manifestation of a man distinguished in some way by mental capacities or other masculine qualities (since when is thinking a purely masculine quality?). Its positive forms are characteristically benevolent, knowledgeable, or understanding; its negative aspects are cruelly demanding, violently tyrannical, seductive, moralistic, or censorious. It can also function, like that anima, as a bridge between the inner and outer worlds.

The mother archetypes are almost inexhaustible—usually some form of maternal aspect, the underworld, womb-like, etc. The most important of this archetype is mothers of the literal sense, followed by those of the figurative. It may also be symbolized in a variety of impersonal forms; paradise of birth, kingdom of God, church, university, city or country, earth, woods, sea, moon, gardens, caves, cooking vessels, certain animals—cow, hare. Evil symbols, in the Western context, include dragons, witches, graves, deep water, and death.

The child archetype also takes many forms—child, god, dwarf, hobbits, elf, animals—monkey—or objects like jewels, chalices, or the golden ball (trickster-like). It represents the original or child-like conditions in the life of the individual or the species, and thus reminds the conscious mind of its origins and helps to keep it aware—a necessary reminder when the consciousness becomes too one-sided, or too willfully progressive, in a manner that threatens to separate the individual from the roots of his or her being. It also signifies the potentiality of future personality development. It anticipates the synthesis of opposites and the attainment of wholeness. Thus it is said to represent the urge and compulsion towards self-realization. This is a reason that so many of the mythical savior gods' symbols are childlike in nature.

The wise old man is the archetype of meaning or spirit. It often appears as grandfather, sage, magician, king, doctor, priest, professor, or any other authority figure. It represents insight, wisdom, cleverness, willingness to help, and moral qualities. His appearance serves to warn of dangers, provide protective gifts, and so on. As with the other archetypes, the wise old man also possesses both good and bad aspects.

Among archetypes, the self is the most important one. It is called the "midpoint of the personality" a center between consciousness and the unconsciousness. It signifies the harmony and balance between the various opposing qualities that make up the psyche. It remains basically incomprehensible, as the ego consciousness cannot grasp this supra-ordinate personality of which the ego is only one element. The symbols of the self can be anything that the ego takes to be a greater totality than itself. Many symbols fall short of expressing the self in its fullest development. Symbols of the self are often manifested in geometrical forms (mandalas) or by the quaternity (any figure with four parts). Prominent human figures which represent the self are figures like Buddha, Christ, Muhammad, etc. This archetype is also represented by the divine child and by various pairs—

father and son, king and queen, god and goddess, or by a hermaphrodite. To Jung the self is a representation of the "god within us."

Another of Jung's terms is theriomorphic symbols, which include powerful animals, such as the dragon, the snake, elephant, lion, and bear, etc. It is also expressed by plants—lotus and rose—and various mythic objects— the Holy Grail, philosopher's stone.

Jung's goal in psychotherapy is self-realization, realization of wholeness and expression, giving form to whatever is observed. He uses traditional names to explain the mind, and says that to know the self, individuals should understand the unique facts that are related to them. This needs to be done separated from prejudice, theoretical assumptions, or generalized knowledge. He explains the teleological significance of having a purpose and meaning related to non-pathological experience, and says that the psychic process is past forces living in the present and movement toward a purpose and goal in the future.

His other concept is synchronicity, which refers to events that occur simultaneously and meaningfully, but are not causal or causally related.

About myth and methodology, Jung says that humans are capable of myth-making. These are deep, and sometimes meaningful, events that are in our fantasy world and will sometimes come up to make up our stories. Each of these may be reflection of some form of absolute in each individual. Therefore, the myths we make up give meaning to existence and help us make some sense of the world within the self. Reason may make it difficult for mythical participation, but mythologizing helps the unconscious become more available to the conscious. Integration is vital for reaching wholeness, and reaching wholeness is the goal of being human. Jung was very interested in Christian as well as Eastern religions, and was captivated by no Western views. He attempted to find similarities between East and West.

For Maslow, self-actualization is a state of reaching full potential. Maslow claimed that authentic mystics are more likely to reach this state of functioning than other people. Mystics are also more likely to have peak experiences, an experience described as having a feeling of ecstasy and oneness with universe. Maslow says that people's choices and values have to come into play for science to be able to function with integrity. He mentions that science without values cannot be used to show that murder is bad. He encourages adopting a broader scientific approach, one in which human motivations are taken into consideration.

Maslow is a contributing force behind transpersonal psychology, which has a focus on the spiritual wellbeing of individuals, acknowledging human values as an important element of this form of psychology. In addition, it aims to find middle grounds between Eastern and Western mysticism, and to combine them with the modern form of psychology.

Jung and Maslow both acknowledged religion as a means that could be used for reaching self-realization and self-actualization, but they both seemed to believe that this means can become unproductive if not used properly. They say that the role of religion is to be a tool for helping individuals reach their fullest state of functioning

(Maslow terms this self-actualization and Jung terms it Wholeness). While Maslow gives us a broader model of human actions and their motivations in life, and how self-realization is an important element of moving up the self-growth process, Jung seems to get into the details of helping us understand how to get to a state of self-realization and what our psyche may be made of.

Wholeness, Self-realization-Individuation

The symbol of unity and totality has been confirmed by history as well as by empirical psychology. There are mandala symbols that happen in dreams of modern humans who have not heard of them otherwise.

When a person goes through the process of individuation, according to Jung, wholeness has to be distinguished from a desire to be perfect. When one realizes the self, one logically understands its innate superiority. This sense of superiority, along with awareness of a whole that is imperfect, can create a sense of conflict. To get to a state of completion, one must learn to experience the self's opposites.

For Jung, finding a meaning and unfolding the self throughout life is an attempt to realize the potential wholeness of personality we all behold. He identifies individuation as becoming an individuate, or one's own self. This seems to be a continuation of self-realization, since to become an individual one has to realize the self. Individuation is to separate one's self from the false identification with the persona and powers of archetypes. This self is a totality of the psyche, conscious, and unconscious. It is an organizing center that tries to maintain a sense of integrity of the personality by maintaining an intra-psychic state of homeostasis.

Individuation is not the same as individualism. The two are usually confused, creating misguidance. Individualism is something that is created by the ego and neglects collective factors. It also focuses too much on an ego-oriented idiosyncrasy. Individuation, on the other hand, is the steady and step-by-step combination and unification of the self through the resolution of consecutive layers of psychological conflict. This is a process of self-realization, self-reflection, and self-knowledge. Jung states that individuation is an "ineluctable psychological necessity" that cannot be shunned; it is one with an aristocratic nature only accessible to those who are predisposed to achieve a higher point. This is exclusive, in a way, to those who are called to it from the beginning. To Jung, the typical mind is satisfied with limited perspectives, which do not consist of the knowledge of the collective unconscious, but at the same time he states that all humans have the capacity to achieve a higher consciousness if they become aware of it.

Jung has written about the individuation process more intensely than many other psychologists. He has used his life experience, his self-analysis, his psychiatric work, as well as his comprehensive studies, to discuss this subject. He believes that individuation usually, for most people, starts within the second part of life. When one compares this with Maslow's concept of self-actualization, it is obvious that these processes both seem to occur in mid-life stages, if other things are moving as they should. Therefore, the second half of life is determined by what the individual has been able to accomplish, mentally and emotionally, during the first half. Some individuals may never get to a point of having a need for self-actualization or to individuate. They might not even become aware that such options exist.

According to Jung, many ideas we form of ourselves are nothing more than a reaction to our fear of facing our wholeness. Self-sacrifice is a fear that lies in the ego and is misidentified by the ego. This fear creates a block for people who want to individuate, but to get to wholeness, this must be passed, and one needs to learn how to get to a supra-human in the psychic archetype. Reaching this stage is a liberating experience. It is, however, not the end but one stage of a process. After this stage, the individual must find the courage to face the object, which is full of projections. At this stage, they must start to excavate, find the enemy within, look at what is truly valuable to them and what is worthless, what is good to them vs. evil, and what they like and dislike. Whatever exists within this world, and the experiences one has with them, are symbols of something that is hidden within the individual who is creating a trans-subjective reality. Therefore, the object is inside the person.

To refer to the concept of ego, at the beginning of life, an infant is completely controlled by the unconscious. At this stage, there is no "me;" there is only instinct. But later on, during the first five years, the ego begins to come out and mold itself into the child's being. This is where the child uses "I" but does not realize that the name attached to it is unique to her. As the child grows, ego gets stronger and the unconscious starts to come into the picture, however not completely. The unconscious is always there, like a guide, especially during the challenges of times when confusion kicks in. In a productive situation, the ego is supposed to evolve and unfold in a healthy way, but this is not an easy task. It needs a lot of courage, awareness and determination to be able to develop a healthy ego. At the end, the goal of a healthy ego is to reach autonomy. An ego is a tool for growth, but in the wrong hands can become a device for damage, damaging the self and anything that may come in contact with the self.

During one's lifetime, the unconscious uses a number of techniques like dreams, fantasies, the body, or interpersonal relationships to open a dialogue with the ego. If the individual can respond to this, and can build a productive relationship with the unconscious, the individuation process can keep on going. If the individual shuts the door to this unconscious and does not pay attention, the ride is in the ego's hand, and the ego is not always the most suitable driver. Therefore, when the individual is unable to enter into a relationship with these hidden forces, the individuation process collapses. In this case, the unconscious can set an obstacle before the person, causing neurosis, which is what Jung explained as a psychological crisis and a "state of disunity." This psychological crisis is due to a state of separation with one's self. According to Jung, neurosis is an effort for self-cure and the psyche's balance.

Jung says that the unconscious appears to have an

intelligence, and a goal in its imposition. The psyche is by nature self-regulating, and its attempt is to balance the individual's psychological state of being. When a person has a hard time becoming accustomed to external or internal reality, the unconscious will react though dreams, fantasies, and synchronistic experiences. This is done to re-establish the lost balance. If there is a feeling of disintegration, the self, which is an inner organizing archetype in the unconscious, will try to reimburse by presenting a sense of unity. For example, images of mandalas that appear in the dreams of a person during a hard time. Other examples of such mandalas would be the Rose windows found in many cathedrals, Ezekiel's vision of wheels within wheels, or Tibetan sand paintings.

When one follows the path of individuation, making mistakes is a part of it. Life will not be complete without mistakes. Some things have to be experienced and cannot simply be read about or be told. But, overall, there is a certain sense of comfort gained in following one's path of individuation. James Hall reports that "when one has worked with the unconscious for a long period of time, one develops the view that the self is like a very wise, very compassionate friend, always concerned to help, but never coercive or excessively judgmental, and possessed of almost infinite patience." If one becomes aware of this state of her being, she can overcome any sense of negative feelings.

Jacobi says that the Jungian individuation process means the conscious realization and incorporation of all the potential that is present within the individual. He further states that, "It is opposed to any kind of conformity and, as a therapeutic factor in analytical work, also demands the rejection of those prefabricated psychic matrices in which people would like to live. It shows that everyone can have his own direction, his mission, and it can make meaningful the lives of those people who suffer from the feeling that they are unable to come up to the collective norms and collective ideals. To those who are not recognized by the collective, who are rejected, and even despised, it can restore their faith in themselves, give them back their human dignity, and assure them their place in the world."

In Maslow's focus on individuation and wholeness, he refers to having values as something that gives individuals the ability to sort out what is important in life and having a focus. He categorized more important values as the "B Values," which are what self-actualized people tend to hold on to more than the lower values. These values include a sense of wholeness, unity, and openness, completion and finality, justice and fairness, aliveness and full functioning, simplicity and structure, quality and richness of life, beauty and art, uniqueness and idiosyncrasy, novelty, playfulness and humor, truth and reality, beauty and pureness, self sufficiency and independence.

Differentiation and Combination

Jung identifies pairs of opposites within an individual's psyche, and states that these are necessary for learning techniques to self-regulate. These include conscious-unconscious, rational-irrational, feminine-masculine, matter-spirit, etc. The discovering and fusion of these opposites is possible, and is the way to one's state of individuation, leading to finding a sense of wholeness. Individuation is a never-ending process in which differentiation and combination are ingredients repeating themselves at a higher and higher level of existence.

Through transcendent function, which is a complex bringing conscious and unconscious together and helping with a transition to a higher plane, an individual's analytical skills can help her differentiate and develop her psyche's components. Through the unconscious forces, the individual is provided with symbols that bring elements into unity, helping her function from a higher level.

According to Jung, individuation is the process of putting together the conscious with the unconscious for the purpose of <u>self-actualization</u>. It is the main goal of development, and is a spiritual and mystical experience. It is the main purpose of Jung's analytical psychology.

The first step toward individuation is differentiation, which is the process of separating each part and psychological function of the psyche, and to be able to acknowledge and understand them. As stated throughout this book, there are three parts to the psyche, which are the ego, the personal conscious, and the collective unconscious. The ego is the conscious mind, the personal unconscious is our life's suppressed memories, and the collective unconscious is shared by all people and is the collective memory of human thought and experiences from ancient times to now. The collective unconscious includes the basic human instincts and the archetypes.

In the integration process of the psyche, individuation is the transformational process through which the conscious is integrated with the personal and collective unconscious. To do that, one has to discover the suppressed memories and heal any psychological trauma. This can be done through psychoanalysis. Then one must be able to understand her thinking pattern and which thoughts create what feelings. Another important step is gaining and increasing knowledge, and developing a sense of determination and self-control.

The individuation process makes a person more true to herself by bringing up the true personality. It makes the person an individual. This has a deep healing effect for the person. It helps people in feeling calmer, more mature, responsible, and in harmony. Such individuals feel and behave as parents or guides to the rest of society. They bring about the concepts of freedom and justice. They hold a collective and broad range of knowledge with a deep understanding of human nature and the bigger picture.

Jung states that our society gets youth ready for the first half of life by providing education, but does not prepare them for the middle age and second half of life. The first half of life focuses mainly on establishing a sense of family and career, while the second half focuses on finding a meaning in life and the individuation process. It gets difficult for people to make a transition between these two if they are not prepared for it. To make the transition successfully and have a fruitful aging, one has to be able to individuate. As I said earlier, Jung's individuation process is similar to Maslow's self-actualization process. Modern psychology defines a successful aging as having generally good mental and physical health, being an active participant in life (being vital), being able to bounce back from stressing factors and challenges (being resilient), and a sense of contentment and happiness.

Some researchers, like Hock and Maddox, have identified two styles to aging; normal and pathological. Normal aging tolerates some form of mental or physical problems and some loss of vitality and resilience, while pathological aging includes a lack of health, vitality, resilience, or happiness. It may also include disorders like insomnia and depression. Pathological aging may happen because of a lack of meaning in life. Meaning is subjective, and cannot be measured the same way for all, but is closely related to a balanced form of happiness.

Overall, awareness is the key to the process of individuation. An individual who has a neurosis, but knows that she's neurotic, is more individuated than the one without this consciousness. If an individual is contradicted by herself and does not know it, she is an illusionist, but if she knows that she contradicts herself, she is walking the individuation process.

According to Jung, humans are innately whole, but lose touch with that foundation. We have to listen to our imagination and dreams to be able to get to know our elements. We need to give expression and learn to harmonize the various components of the psyche. If we understand our uniqueness, we can learn about our true self. Each individual has a certain nature that can be discovered through the unity of conscious and unconscious. If that task is not accomplished, the person is jamming her growth and may even experience sick feelings.

Every person has a story which needs to be discovered. Sometimes, what passes for "normal" is the very same force which can destroy an individual's personality. When trying to be "normal" according to external and stereotypical images goes against one's inner nature, it forms pathology. For Jung, life is an unlimited mystery which is little understood.

Psychological Types

The first of Jung's psychological types are introversion and extroversion. Jung describes the process of individuation occurring in two phases of youth and middle age for individuals walking normally through the path of life. The youth age needs an extroverted outlook to life in which the libido is directed toward outside world and material things, including marriage, career, business, education, relationships, etc.

The transition between this stage and the next one occurs around ages 35 to 40. This is the time in which the individual finds a need to re-examine values she holds and to broaden her views of life and her ideas. This is the phase in which a sense of introversion emerges, in which the individual's attention is centered more toward the internal world and the development of her psyche. This is where wisdom and general knowledge come into play. It has its own principles, moving toward self-realization and the blending of opposites.

Jung's categorizations include sensation and intuition,

which are defined as irrational since both deliver perceptions that are not based on reason. Sensation is the process of recognizing physical stimuli from both the outside world and the inside organic changes and signals. It is the opposite of intuition, which has the role of mediating perceptions in an unconscious way. Intuition contains a whole and complete knowledge that brings about certainty if accessed correctly.

The next of Jung's categorizations are thinking and feeling, which are the theoretical relationships of psychic content. There are two levels to thinking, active and passive. An active way of thinking has a goal of coming to some form of judgment or decision, while a passive one is more of an intuitive form of thinking, in which abstract links seem to set themselves up, creating judgments opposite to one's intention.

These two types of thinking are not similar to what some define as an associative thinking. One role of associative thinking is to produce ideas, not to form links or come up with judgments and decisions. Jung says that only directed thinking is rational, since undirected thinking lies in the unconscious, and he does not consider associative thinking a form of thinking at all.

Thinking is something that is the opposite of feeling. When we think, we are reacting to our psychic content with a subjective judgment of values. If it is affected by reflection and is in tune with reason, then it can be considered rational.

For Jung, a state of an ideal self would be a place in which an individual develops both extraversion and introversion, along with the functions of sensation and intuition, thinking and feeling, and perceiving and judging. If one of these is isolated, it falls into the unconsciousness and turns into the inferior function, while its opposing force turns into a superior one, remaining in the conscious behavioral pattern. The inferior function becomes more and more inaccessible as it is being neglected.

Self-actualization

Maslow says, "Self-actualization is the intrinsic growth of what is already in the organism, or more accurately, of what the organism is." Maslow studied healthy people during about 20 years of his investigation of talents and potentials. His basic principles are:

A normal personality is distinguished by unity, integration, consistency, and coherence. A natural state of being is organized, whereas a pathological one is disorganized. Organization brings efficiency.

The organism can be studied by distinguishing its parts, but no part can be studied separately. The whole functions according to laws that cannot be found in the parts.

The organism has one superior drive, and that is self-actualization. Individuals struggle on a regular basis to realize this inherent potential.

Normal growth cannot be accomplished by being influenced by the external environment. If the individual is exposed to a suitable environment and is allowed to unfold, her innate potential will produce a healthy and incorporated personality.

The complete study of one person can be more beneficial than that of many people's isolated psychological functions.

To recover a human being, we cannot focus on behaviorism or psychoanalysis alone; these deal with the darker side of the individual. In addition to that, we must provide answers for questions like values, individuality, consciousness, meaning, purpose, ethical and moral values, and the higher end of human nature.

Humans are innately good, not evil.

Psychopathology commonly results from the rejection, disturbance, or distortion of our essential nature.

Healing or therapy of any kind should be a tool of renovating a sense of self-actualization in accordance with the individual's inner nature.

When the individual's basic needs have been met, higher level needs, including the need for self-actualization, surface. If this need is ignored, a sense of discontent and agitation will be seeded in the individual. A musician must make music, an artist must paint, a poet must write, a scientist must investigate. What people can be, they must be.

Maslow's hierarchy of needs

1) Physiological: hunger, thirst, bodily comforts, homeostasis, etc.
2) Safety and security: out of danger, feeling of stability (cultural, societal, financial, environmental)
3) Belongingness and love: healthy interactions and connections, be accepted
4) Esteem: externally by achieving, being competent, gaining approval and recognition, or internally by having a sense of inner contentment with one's self.
5) Cognitive: to know, to understand, and explore;
6) Aesthetic: artistic pleasures, symmetry, order, and beauty
7) Self-actualization: to find self-fulfillment, to have self-control and control over life, and realize one's potential
8) Self-transcendence: to connect to something beyond the ego, a bigger existence, a sense of selflessness, or to help others find self-fulfillment and realize their potential.

According to Maslow, as humans get closer to self-actualization and self-transcendence, they develop more wisdom. This wisdom gives them an instinctive knowledge of how to go about their lives. Daniels says that Maslow's fundamental assumption of the highest levels of self-actualization and transcendence may well be his most crucial contribution to the study of human motivation.

Norwood states that Maslow's hierarchy can be a tool

to explain why individuals seek information at different levels. Individuals at the lower levels seem to be looking for coping information to find ways to meet their basic needs, while those at the safety level may seek helping information to see how they can feel safe and secure. Then there is enlightening information-seeking behavior, which is done by individuals who search to meet their need for belonging or connection to others.

Empowering information is searched for by individuals at the esteem level to find out how their ego can be developed. When individuals are at the growth level of cognitive, aesthetic, and self-actualization, they search for edifying information.

There are other studies which categorize human needs that have some similarities and some differences with Maslow's. William James reported that there are three levels of human needs; material (physiological, safety), social (belongingness, esteem), and spiritual. Mathes stated that the three levels are physiological, belongingness, and self-actualization.

Alderfer shaped an analogous hierarchy, consisting of existence, relatedness, and growth (ERG theory).

Existence: material and psychological desires; when divided, one person's gain is another's loss, if resources are limited.

Relatedness: relationships with significant others, satisfied by mutually sharing thoughts and feelings; acceptance, confirmation, understanding, and influence.

Growth: driving a person to make creative or productive influences on herself or her surroundings, satisfied through using her capabilities in engaging problems; creates a greater sense of wholeness and fullness as a human being.

Maslow understood that his hierarchy does not apply to all personality types in the same way. For example, when considering the introversion and extroversion aspects of personality, and incorporating Maslow's model with that of Alderfer, the following three levels can be included; self, other, and growth.

Self (existence): for introversion, it is the physiological, biological, and basic emotional needs; for extroversion, it is the sense of connectedness and security.

Other (relatedness): for introversion it is the personal identification with the group, significant others (belongingness); for extroversion it is the value of person by group (esteem).

Growth: for introversion it is self-actualization (development of competencies like knowledge, attitudes, and skills; and development of character); for extroversion it is transcendence (assisting in the development of others' competencies and character; relationships to the unknown.

Characteristics of self-actualized individuals

Self-actualized people are more realistic and logical, have a well-organized perception of reality, have a superior ability to reason, and are more capable of seeing the truth. They have the ability to accept themselves, and, as a result, others, enjoy themselves without regret or apology, are spontaneous, simplistic, and have autonomous ethical values. They are motivated by a continual sense of growth. They focus on problems on a broader perspective, have a mission in life which takes a lot of their focus and gives them a reason to live meaningfully, are devoted to duty, and lack unreasonable worry. They have a need for privacy and being alone while not feeling lonely, are self-starters, responsible, and own their own behaviors. They are autonomous, and have moved above, and are independent of, any culture and environmental conditioning. They are stable in hard times, self-contained, and content. They have a unique sense of appreciation of life and people which is not based on stereotypical imposition. They appreciate the basic good of life, live in the moment while planning for the future, and are transcending and spiritual. They live their life to the fullest.

In interpersonal relations, self-actualized individuals have profound intimate relationships with a few, and are capable of greater love than others consider possible. They show genuine affection and friendliness toward most everyone, which comes naturally. They have independent values and attitudes, are able to learn from anyone, and are humble and friendly toward others, regardless of class, beliefs, education level, race, color, religion, or any other sort of material categorization. They are creative and resistant to enculturation. They are painfully aware of their own imperfections, joyfully aware of their growth process, and feel the pain when it is real. They have ways of merging opposites to bring a third higher phenomenon into existence.

Maslow says there are two processes necessary for self-actualization: self-exploration and action. The deeper the self-exploration, the closer one comes to self-actualization.

Self-actualized individuals have peak experiences. Maslow states, "Feelings of limitless horizons opening up to the vision, the feeling of being simultaneously more powerful and also more helpless than one ever was before, the feeling of ecstasy and wonder and awe, the loss of placement in time and space, with, finally, the conviction that something extremely important and valuable had happened, so that the subject was to some extent transformed and strengthened even in his daily life by such experiences."

Maslow asked his subjects to think of the most amazing experiences of their lives, their happiest moments, the ones in which they felt a sense of ecstasy; moments of bliss from listening to a certain music or being touched by a book or creative art. He found that individuals who go through peak experiences feel more integrated and one with the world, are more in charge of their own lives, are less aware of space and time, enjoy simplicity, are more perceptive and self-determined, and are more playful.

Maslow did biographical analyses of his subjects to come up with what self-actualization means. He started his process by choosing a variety of people, including some historical figures and people he knew, who he thought met the general standards of self-actualization. He searched into their biographies, writings, and the acts and words of those he knew personally. He developed a list of qualities that seemed characteristic of these people as opposed to the great mass of people.

Other characteristics that Maslow came up with for the self-actualized included being reality-centered, meaning that they could distinguish between a genuine act vs. what is dishonest and not well-intended. In addition, these people have a healthy way of solving problems and demanding solutions, and do not look at it as a personal trouble to be engulfed by. They also perceive the journey of life to be more important than the ends and means that are used to walk through that journey.

The self-actualizers also had a different way of relating to others. First, they take pleasure in seclusion and are comfortable being alone. In addition, they enjoy deep personal connections with a few rather than many shallow ones. They focus on quality rather than quantity. They don't overwhelm themselves with too many distractions, and have learned ways to focus on a few deep relationships.

They care about autonomy, and are independent of social and physical needs. They are not susceptible to social pressure to fit in. They don't conform to what their inner core does not value. They have a sense of social interest, compassion, and humanity. In addition, they have a strong ethic that is spiritual, but seldom based on conventionally religious and ritualistic beliefs.

Self-actualized individuals have a profound sense of appreciation for things, even simple ones, which they look upon with wonder. They are creative, inventive, and original. Maslow says that self-actualized people are not perfect, but are aware of their weaknesses and crave self-improvement. One of the most common weaknesses is a sense of anxiety and guilt, which even though reasonable and not neurotic, can interfere with their creativity. This anxiety and fear can be due to their profound awareness of the world and their self. The other weakness is that these people can be overly kind; all the way to making themselves look absentminded.

To become self-actualized, one needs to learn to experience things fully and selflessly, one needs to learn to concentrate on what matters, simple or complex, and one needs to let it totally attract one's being. One has to learn that life is an endless process of choosing between what feels safe, which comes out of fear, or what risks one needs to take to make progress in life. If one learns to make the second choice, it will be a more productive life. One has to let her self emerge, focusing from a center and internal knowing rather than the external conditioning of what to think, how to feel, what to say, and how to be. One needs to become true to her self, and express herself the way she is. One has to learn to take responsibility for her life and be accountable for any mistakes. One has to learn to listen to her own signals and stand out, even if alone. One has to learn to use her intelligence and do well and be productive in many areas of life. The more skills, the more capable one becomes. One needs to learn who she is, what she likes and does not, what is good or bad for her, where she is heading in life, and what goals she has. She needs to identify defenses and find the courage to give up what does not work. At the end, humans have an internal drive to become the best possible person they can be.

Maslow states,"...he has within him a pressure toward unity of personality, toward spontaneous expressiveness, toward full individuality and identity, toward seeing the truth rather than being blind, toward being creative, toward being good, and a lot else. That is, the human being is so constructed that he presses toward what most people would call good values, toward serenity, kindness, courage, honesty, love, unselfishness, and goodness."

He further states, "The state of being without a system of values is psychopathogenic, we are learning. The human being needs a framework of values, a philosophy of life, a religion or religion-surrogate to live by and understand by, in about the same sense he needs sunlight, calcium, or love. This I have called the 'cognitive need to understand.' The value-illnesses which result from valuelessness are variously called anhedonia, anomie, apathy, amorality, hopelessness, cynicism, etc., and can become somatic illness as well. Historically, we are in a value interregnum in which all externally-given value systems have proven failures (political, economic, religious, etc.); e.g., nothing is worth dying for. What man needs but doesn't have, he seeks for unceasingly, and he becomes dangerously ready to jump at any hope, good or bad. The cure for this disease is obvious. We need a validated, usable system of human values that we can believe in and devote ourselves to (be willing to die for), because they are true rather than because we are exhorted to "believe and have faith." Such an empirically-based Weltanschauung seems now to be a real possibility, at least in theoretical outline."

Being moral comes naturally, but the key is to learn how to think, be honest, open, and authentic. Maslow says, "Pure spontaneity consists of free, uninhibited, uncontrolled, trusting, unpremeditated expression of the self, i.e., of the psychic forces, with minimal interference by consciousness. Control, will, caution, self-criticism, measure, and deliberateness are the brakes upon this expression, made intrinsically necessary by the laws of the social and natural world and, secondarily, made necessary by the fear of the psyche itself." And, "This ability of healthier people to dip into the unconscious and preconscious, to use and value their primary processes instead of fearing them, to accept their impulses instead of always controlling them, to be able to regress voluntarily without fear, turns out to be one of the main conditions of creativity." He goes on to say, "This development toward the concept of a healthy unconscious, and of a healthy irrationality, sharpens our awareness of the limitations of purely abstract thinking, of verbal thinking and of analytic thinking. If our hope is to describe the world fully, a place is necessary for preverbal, ineffable, metaphorical, primary process, concrete-experience, intuitive and esthetic types of cognition, for there are certain aspects of reality which can be cognized in no other way."

According to Maslow, we need to inner-explore and act to be able to walk toward self-actualization. He says, "An important existential problem is posed by the fact that self-actualizing persons (and all people in their peak-experiences) occasionally live out-of-time and out-of-the-world (atemporal and aspatial) even though mostly they must live in the outer world. Living in the inner psychic world (which is ruled by psychic laws and not by the laws of outer-reality), i.e., the world of experience, of emotion, of wishes and fears and hopes, of love of poetry, art, and fantasy, is different from living in and adapting to the non-psychic reality which runs by laws he never made and which are not essential to his nature, even though he has to live by them. (He could, after all, live in other kinds of worlds, as any science fiction fan knows.) The person who is not afraid of this inner, psychic world can enjoy it to such an extent that it may be called Heaven by contrast with the more effortful, fatiguing, externally responsible world of "reality," of striving and coping, of right and wrong, of truth and falsehood. This is true even though the healthier person can also adapt more easily and enjoyably to the "real" world, and has better 'reality testing,' i.e., doesn't confuse it with his inner psychic world."

Self-actualized people need the following to feel content with their life: truth, goodness, beauty, unity and wholeness, and transcendence of opposites, vitality, being unique, consistency, completion, justice and order, simplicity, effortlessness, playfulness, self-sufficiency, and having a meaning in life. If they don't get these needs fulfilled, they may experience feelings of depression, despair, disgust, and alienation, or a degree of cynicism.

General Comparison of Different Theorists

Jung disagreed with Freud's overemphasis on humans' lower animal nature and not the importance of aspirations. Jung described a predisposition toward higher values and a need for spiritual fulfillment. Jung's definition of self-actualization is a congruent, balanced, and mature personality.

Maslow says, "I never met Freud or Jung." Then he writes, "But I did meet with Adler in his home, where he used to run Friday night seminars, and I had many conversations with him... As for many of the others, I sought them out—people like Erich Fromm and Karen Horney and Ruth Benedict and Max Wertheimer and the like... I think it's fair to say that I have had the best teachers, both formal and informal, of any person who even lived, just because of the historical accident of being in New York City when the very cream of European intellect was migrating away from Hitler. New York City in those days was simply fantastic. There has been nothing like it since Athens." Then he says, "And I think I knew every one of them more or less well. The ones that I have mentioned in my prefaces are the ones I felt so grateful to and knew most closely. I cannot say that any one of them was any more important than any other. I was just learning from everybody and from anybody who had anything to teach me...I learned from all of them... So I could not be said to be a Goldsteinian nor a Frommian to join any of these parochial and sectarian organizations. I learned from all of them and refused to close any doors."

The predisposition of humans for self-actualization has been reported by thinkers like Aristotle and Bergson, to many psychoanalyst and psychiatrists who have identified self-actualization as an essential factor to being a human. These include people like Fromm, May, Rogers, Rank, Horney, Goldstein, and of course Jung.

Allport states that there is "significant revolution that is occurring." He makes reference to an "attitudinal therapy." This is a healthy evolution from Freudian concepts; works of such men as Adler, Jung, Hartmen, Horney, Erickson, Fromm, Goldstein, Rogers, and Maslow. Allport states, "Only now, at long last, are the laws of mental illness and health being discovered, and even today relatively few people know that such laws exist."

What theorists like Maslow, Jung, and Wilber, among others, seem to have in common is trying to offer an alternative to the traditional views and practices of religion. Jung was one of the ones most determined to provide a detailed explanation of Christianity, and, in a way, to transform it. He stated that psychology can give a more rational approach to the thirst for religion in humans. Reiff states that Jung tried to replace the institutional religion that no longer served its purpose with his own private myth.

Jung wants people to not be followers of others, but of their own unique core. He encouraged those who were not completed by their religion to find their own vision and focus on it. To find a place where there is faith. He disregarded the traditional form of Churches and some of their morals and their application to the modern life, and attempted to translate the God into terms like "suprahistorical" and "transcultural" archetypes that are present in everyone. He further states that Christianity, or the "Christ archetype", is not productive anymore because it has lost its shine and emotional benefits. As a result of that, the Western world has failed to connect her archetypes and is left with an unbalanced psyche. It is worth noting that Jung focused on Christianity because he was a practicing Christian, and was very knowledgeable about it. But his statements can have applications to other religions as well. It seems like a worldwide problem that religious concepts are not evolving fast enough to satisfy the thirst of an evolved mind, and if something does not come into play to replace it, people will feel more and more a sense of loss and conflict. Again, Jung states that psychology would be that replacement. It is a channel for a humans' creative impulse. Jung labels a human as "himself an entire church," a combination of different archetypes capable of achieving wholeness, and therefore never really lonely.

Once a person takes in psychology and starts a self-transformation process, examining his own personality and all elements related to it, she can find a way to a psychological equilibrium. The more she discovers herself, the more she can gain access to her unconscious.

Maslow believes that every religion has a fundamental similarity. He explains religion as "an effort to communicate peak experiences to non-peakers." He states that all religions should make compromises and work together to come up with a general belief system which is based on "whatever it is that peak experiences teach in common." This totality is the "core religious experience or transcendent experience."

Maslow says that an important part of religion is the process of individuation; to become what one is supposed to be. Another key factor to a religious experience is the peak experience during which one feels united with the whole, has a sense of purpose and sees the parts as equal. It needs "tremendous concentration," along with an "egoless" tactile perception. A person who experiences peak experience becomes fearless of death, and sees life as an endless process. The polarity becomes balanced, and the inner self feels unique and valuable. Maslow, similar to Jung, believes that evil has its own place and purpose in the world; it gives notice to good.

Wilber's model of personality has no specific boundary, and has many layers to it. He calls it the spectrum of consciousness, which is like beams of light going through a prism. The mind level is the deepest level of reality, something like an infinite and eternal ocean. At this level, the individual is one with the whole; this is the only true state of consciousness, a sense of selflessness, but with a sense of awareness of an identity; functioning from the whole, but being aware of the parts. Wilber would encourage individuals to overcome their archetypes and solve the duality of subject and object. The individual's boundaries are unlimited, but she is not aware of it. The task would be to become aware of this ocean.

Healing would be done one step at a time, walking through the levels, and changing a partial view of what is real to a broader view. This healing process is unique and personal.

Maslow states that only after individuals have found a way to deal with their ego needs can they truly and sincerely work for their fellow humans. Whatever else we, as humans, do before that, no matter how we label it, may be nothing more than satisfying our own needs, the need for financial or emotional security, power, recognition, etc.

After Jung, Maslow is the most often cited psychologist in the literature. Maslow's focus on the self-actualized and healthy person is similar to Rogers' terminology of a fully functioning individual. Rogers explains actualization of the self as a process by which the person achieves her ideal self by continuously changing and being in touch with her feelings and emotions throughout life.

In today's psychology, we see more and more focus on positive aspects of a person rather than pathologies and problems. For example, Adler's focus on the creative self and social interest, Jung's self-realization, Erikson's psychological stages, Maslow's self-actualization, and existentialist concepts like those of Seligman. There also seems to be more focus on positive traits like hopefulness, caring, responsibility, resilience, creativity, and wisdom. Further, it is obvious that psychological wellbeing is moving beyond the ego aspects and into the spiritual areas, as well.

Adler's view of a mentally healthy individual is the one who meets the chores of life with adaptable problem-solving skills that take into account the wellbeing of others. He also focused on a goal of optimal development as a point on the way to becoming mentally healthy.

One of the arguments that Wilber makes, based on summary of a number of scholars' work, is that Western psychology has focused almost entirely on the area of personal development from an egoistic point of view, while the Eastern psychology has focused entirely on transpersonal development. He goes on to credit a number of scholars who have focused on both aspects equally. For example, Gustav Fechner, who originated experimental psychology, but who focused on the concept that the material world is an expression of the divine consciousness. Another important figure was Baldwin, who has a transpersonal concept. Wilber also mentions Maslow for his work focusing on both aspects of psychology.

Maslow promotes the idea that individuals should create an optimal environment for themselves that makes it possible for them to go through the process of personal and spiritual growth. These "eupsychian environments" should include similar-minded people who share the same values and same concepts of transpersonal development, in which the individuals are focused on self-growth and fruitfulness on the same level, in which each participant supports and provides the conditions allowing each other to bring out defenses and emerge into new ways of being.

The word eupsychian (pronounced "you-sigh-key-un") was coined by Maslow. It comes from *eu* meaning *good* (i.e. *eu*phoria) and *psyche* meaning, basically, *mind* or *soul*. So *eupsychian* essentially means "having a good mind/soul" or "toward a good mind/soul."

Jung says, "…very personal nature and an irresistible influence. I call it 'God'." He then says, "I don't believe, but I do know of a power of a very personal nature and an irresistible influence. I call it 'God.'" From Jung's perspective, psychology's concern is not to prove or deny religious ideas, but with the fact that those ideas do exist.

Jung studied religious traditions of the East and the West, and techniques like yoga and meditation, extensively. Jung says the Eastern mind is more introverted, which has a tendency to get into the psyche and the source of creation, while the Western mind is more extroverted, which has a longing to be lifted up in the outer reality. Neither mind is fully able to understand the other if it does not cultivate and nurture both aspects of introversion and extroversion. If there is too much focus on one and not the other, the Eastern mind may seem antisocial and negligent to the Westerner, while to the Easterner the Westerner's mind seems engulfed in illusions and materialistic desires that slave her to the world of suffering.

Jung found meanings for many religious symbols, and related them to psychological states. For example, archetypes of Gods dying young relate the idea of an individual dying to the limited ego with which we identify to be the true self. Another example would be that the religious symbols of fish and serpent creatures that appear to be suddenly emerging from the depth represent a psychological level of emergence from unconscious to full awareness. Another example would be the Christian trinity; he saw a three stage psychological maturation process of individuation in this symbol. The first state is the father, and it is when the psyche is in its beginning stage of undifferentiated wholeness, then the son which represents the transformation state, and the last stage is the eternal holy existence.

Jung describes a symbol as, "A term, a name, or even a picture that may be familiar in daily life, yet that possesses specific connotations in addition to its conventional and obvious meaning. It implies something vague, unknown, or hidden from us." He explains symbols as emerging from the unconscious which hold a universal place, for example, geometric shapes such as the cross, the triangle, the crescent, the star, the square, the pyramid, and the circle. These symbols are derived from the unconscious, and are like a key unlocking what was once identified as a mystery. Therefore, mystery is, after all, nothing more than an undiscovered truth. Jung's explanations are similar to religious beliefs that some form of meditation or thought process, or religious symbols, or any form of deep meaningful artistry, can help alter internal experiences inaccessible to conscious awareness.

Jung says that individuals are innately whole, but they lose touch with that truth. By listening to our dreams and imaginations and the messages they may bring, and through listening to the messages of our dreams and waking imagination, we can contact and reintegrate our different parts. The goal of life is individuation, the process of coming to know, giving expression to, and harmonizing the various components of the psyche. If we realize our uniqueness, we can undertake a process of individuation and tap into our true self. Each human being has a specific nature and calling which is uniquely his or her own, and unless these are fulfilled through a union of conscious and unconscious, the person can become sick.

Jung explains that everyone has a story, and if this story is denied or rejected it creates some form of disorganization within the person. When the person starts to discover her own story, assimilation starts to come into play. Another of Jung's statements is that what is labeled "normal" in society may be the very same factor that can crush an individual's personality. When trying to be "normal" according to other people's rules violates the person's inner nature, it can create pathology. He identifies life as a mystery, of which we know very little, and says that we need to pay attention to our unconscious because it is the driving force, whether we want it to be or not. All products the unconscious are symbolic and have a message for us, if we focus.

Jung believes that individuals must take steps in sequential order to get in touch with their self, and to individuate. The first step to individuation is differentiation. It is to distinguish and separate each part, or psychological function, of the <u>psyche</u> in order to consciously access and understand them.

This starts with understanding one's shadow and anima-animus. Most people will be tempted to leave out working on the shadow and go right ahead to what feels more comfortable, but that will not do the work. We have to clean the mirror first, to see a true reflection of who we are, before we can start any work. If we don't do that, the shadow can make our vision of the truth hazy.

Jung referred to the first step as "the First Act of Courage." It is to acknowledge that the shadow exists, and to step out of avoidance and denial. It may sound straightforward, but many people do not feel comfortable admitting that there is a dark side to their nature. At the end, we all have to understand that what we disown in ourselves will be projected externally, consciously or unconsciously.

When we are looking into the shadow, one clue to look for is projection of the content of shadow. It is seeing the degree of negative emotion that is provoked by some external factor, like other people, whether it is a behavior or just the way someone looks. A feeling and an emotion that is associated with that particular external factor can be evaluated.

Jung says that feeling is a task which assesses, while an emotion is an outcome, a response. When discovering our shadow, we must evaluate our feelings and emotions while interacting with the outside world. For example, if we are not greatly upset, but are labeling something as bad, we may experience a sense of regret or pity. But if the emotion is strong, we may self-reflect to see what it is we see in the other that is giving us such a strong feeling that may be a reflection of us. However, not all projection is negative. For example, there is a form of anger which motivates social action for change.

When we start discovering and understanding our shadow, we start to feel lighter. This lightness starts to reflect itself throughout our interactions with the external world, including interactions with others. We get more comfortable and less harmful, since we do not project so much of a negative nature outward. Another factor worth noting is the term "Golden Shadow," meaning the things of value that we have disowned and placed in the shadow, like aptitudes and qualities that can be productive if accessed. The problem with shadow work is confronting frightening, or maybe even shameful, aspects of our self.

Another important factor to consider, in psychological terms, is complexes. These are a group of unconscious associations and conflicting beliefs that stand on their own like a fragmented identity. Complexes are strong unconscious impulses, and are detectable by a behavior that is confusing or hard to explain. Complexes like "guilt complex" deplete the energy from the conscious ego. Anything unconscious can be projected onto others.

In order for us to become aware individuals, we need to improve and speed up the process of logical thinking when dealing with life's problems. We need to start training ourselves with deep thinking and understanding that there is a full knowledge base that is accessible intuitively to all of us. We also have to be aware of our conditioning, habits, and fight or flight emotional reactions, since they may create restraint.

There are, and always have been, people of high-ranking scholarly views who have found spirituality without being involved in traditional religion. This seems to be growing. Erich Fromm states that, "It is not true that we have to give up the concern for the soul if we do not accept the tenets of religion." Our era is marked by a time of spiritual disorientation. Jung commented that, "We have stripped all things of their mystery and luminosity; nothing is holy any longer."

Existential psychologists like Franks have underlined that fact that the roots of today's conflict and distress are the roots of today's pathologies. Therefore, psychology cannot ignore the spiritual needs of individuals. Jung says that he was able to help cure only the patients in their midlife who were able to pick up a spiritual direction in life. In addition, transpersonal psychologists like Wilber and Vaughan, among others, have made attempts to bring attention to this vital but ignored area of psychology. Maslow says that, "The human being needs a framework of values, a philosophy of life, a religion or region-surrogate, to live by and understand by, in about the same sense that he needs sunlight, calcium, or love."

Other writers who looked at spirituality from a logical and systematic perspective are William James, Rudolph Otto, John Dewey, Gordon Allport, Mircea Eliade, Martin Buber, Erich Fromm, and Viktor Frankl, to name a few.

Spirituality is a multidimensional complex and cannot be defined in simplistic terminology. As I said earlier in this book, Maslow's impression of traditional and organized religion was not a favorable one. His concern was that a genuine sense of spirituality is missing. He states that, "I want to demonstrate that spiritual values have naturalistic meaning, that they are not exclusive possessions of organized churches, that they do not need supernatural concepts to validate them, that they are well within the jurisdiction of a suitably enlarged science, and that therefore they are the general responsibility of all mankind. Maslow, like Dewey, viewed spirituality as a human experience.

Studies indicate that a small number of people who consider spirituality to be personally relevant participated in traditional religion. For example, Shafranske and Malony's study reports that while 71% of people report spirituality being relevant, only 9% reported a high level of involvement with traditional religious settings and 74% reported that organized religion was not their main source of spirituality.

Jung states that there is a universal belief in spirit, which is a direct expression of the complex structure of our unconscious. Through complexes (the living units of the unconscious psyche), we are able to figure out the existence and foundation of spirit.

Conclusion

This book's attempt was to compare and bring together a number of views related to transpersonal psychology. When it comes to psychology and its developmental stages, psychologists have looked at all areas of life from conception to death dividing it into categories. Psychologists like Piaget, Freud, and Erickson are still being mentioned in an attempt to explain the early stages of life but, in general, there is much greater focus on the later areas of life into the second part of adulthood.

As time moves forward, the need for finding root oriented answers to the thirst for understanding spirituality increases. The authentic spiritual need usually arises during the adulthood stage of life.

When it comes to the history of humans trying to understand their place in and connection to life and transpersonal experiences, these have always been a part of humans' existence and have been present as long as the thought process came to be. In addition, thought process and the need for understanding are evolving together; as the former expands, the later deepens. With that comes transpersonal psychology.

Transpersonal psychology studies spiritual aspects of individuals' experiences; in addition, it focuses on humans' highest potential, transcendent and spiritual dimensions of humanity, peak experiences, and the possibility of development beyond the traditional ego boundaries. It attempts to find a bridge of understanding between spirituality and psychology. It also focuses on the self beyond the ego or personal aspect into deeper levels of consciousness and the connections with the bigger picture of existence. Transpersonal psychology has created a new dimension suggesting an area of life goal in which one wants to experience self transformation and transcendence. This goal is a continuous process of expansion.

Thinkers like Carl Jung, Roberto Assagioli, and Abraham Maslow among others are contributing scholars to this school of thought. Out of the other school of psychology including psychoanalysis, behaviorism, and humanistic ones; transpersonal psychology seems to be the one focusing the most on a whole spectrum of being a human integrating other school of thoughts.

While general psychology is more focused on a range of human experience from severe dysfunction to normal and healthy functioning, transpersonal psychology goes beyond this spectrum by adding a multimodal dimension to human experience. Exceptional higher functioning and experiences, genuineness to self, mystical experiences, higher states of consciousness, and higher potential as human beings are some of the areas transpersonal psychology is attempting to explore. It combines various areas of psychology in addition to the science of cognition, consciousness, social and cultural concepts and history, multimodal health practices, literature, art, and spiritual wisdom to come up with theories explaining human nature. It is not limited to one mode of explaining what it means to have a humanly experience but brings different school of thoughts together, it does not separate but tries to find commonality. Furthermore, as mentioned before, transpersonal psychology's aim is to combine modern psychology with other disciplines including general science, politics, education, anthropology, history, sociology, literary studies, religious studies, biology and physics to bring answers.

Human psyche is spiritual by nature. Finding an inner balance and harmony is important in becoming a fully functioning human reaching that unique full potential. Relying too heavily on logic and natural science or, on the other side of the spectrum, relying too much on realms that are not within the logical mode of explanations, will only create more confusion. There has to be a midpoint of connection and balance between rationality and intuition to help individuals discover and make sense of who they are and how they are connected to life. This balance is important for the individuation process and becoming a whole person. A person functioning from a wholeness point of being is able to integrate her consciousness with the unconscious while still having a sense of conscious autonomy.

Transpersonal psychology tries to combine psychology and spirituality bringing mystical and spiritual disciplines into the formula of understanding human's psyche. It is based on non duality and the recognition that any element is a part of a whole and that concept includes humans. It goes beyond psychological explanations that are based solely on mechanism, reductionist views, and separations. Additionally, it views individuals as having a sense of deeper identity which is broad and unified with a whole which is the source, it future explains that there is a basic goodness within all individuals.

Transpersonal psychology is not based on a belief system and does not have an institutional structure but has a goal of guiding individuals through a personal spiritual experience which is rooted in self discovery and self knowledge. Furthermore, it offers insight through research and evaluation of findings. It is not a religion or an ideology or some form of metaphysics. It is, however, based on a sense of connectedness with the deeper self, nature, and social and interpersonal dimensions. As mentioned, it encourages an inner balance between rationality and intuition, and integrative awareness and contemplation.

Practices of transpersonal psychology include self reflection and meditation, mindfulness, self evaluation and observation, self realization, and gathering knowledge all of which can open the door to a form of self liberation which is an internal state of freedom, an inner peace and calm which comes from a state of self control and awareness. These practices are more related to human nature and the depth it is in. Psychology needs to evolve continuously to bring answers to deeper elements of human existence such as altered states of consciousness, spirituality and religious attractions.

Among pioneers of transpersonal psychology are Carl Gustav Jung who introduced collective unconscious and archetypes and tried to understand and explain religious archetypes from a psychological perspective. Another pioneer is Abraham Maslow whose study of self actualization, peak experiences, and self transcendence brought humanistic psychology as well as transpersonal psychology into form. Another would be Roberto Assagioli who is the founder of psychosynthesis, a transpersonally based approach to therapy and personal growth. And Ken Wilber who is currently the leading theorist in transpersonal psychology, who has developed a model of the evolution of consciousness that integrates the philosophies and psychologies of West and East, ancient and modern.

References

Alderfer, C. (1972). Existence, Relatedness, & Growth. New York: Free Press.

Allport, G. (1960). Personality and Social Encounter: Selected Essays. New York: Beacon Press.

Allport, G. (1961). Pattern and Growth in Personality. New York: Holt, Rinehart, and Winston.

Chodorow, J. (1991). Dance Therapy and Depth Psychology. London: Routledge.

Daniels, M. (2001). *Maslow's Concept of Self-actualization*. Retrieved February 2004, from http://www.mdani. demon.co.uk/archive/MDMaslow.htm

Davidson, D. (1966). Transference as a Form of Active Imagination. In M. Fordham et al., eds., Technique in Jungian analysis. London: Heinemann, 1974.

Franken, R. (2001). *Human Motivation* (5th ed.). Pacific Grove, CA: Brooks/Cole.

Hopcke, R. H. (1989). A Guided Tour of the Collected Works of C. G. Jung. Boston: Shambhala.

Hall, J. A. (1983). Jungian Dream Interpretation: A Handbook of Theory and Practice. Toronto: Inner City.

Huitt, W. (2004). Maslow's Hierarchy of Heeds. Educational Psychology Interactive. Valdosta, GA: Valdosta State University. Retrieved [date] from, http://chiron.valdosta.edu/whuitt/col/regsys/maslow.html

Johnson, R. (1986). Inner Work: Using Dreams and Active Imagination for Personal Growth. San Francisco: Harper.

Jung, C. G. (1963). Memories, Dreams, Reflections, trans. R. and C. Winston, ed. A. Jaffé. New *York: Pantheon.*

Jung, C. G. (1962). Symbols of Transformation: An Analysis of the Prelude to a Case of Schizophrenia (Vol. 2, R. F. C. Hull, Trans.). New York: Harper & Brothers.

Jung, C. G. (1989a). *Memories, Dreams, Reflections* (Rev. ed., C. Winston & R. Winston, Trans.) (A. Jaffe, Ed.). New York: Random House, Inc.

Jung, C. G. (1989b). *Psychology and Religion: West and East* (2nd ed., R. F. C. Hull, Trans.). Princeton, NJ: Princeton University Press.

Kalff, D. (1980). Sandplay: A Psychotherapeutic Approach to the Psyche. Santa Monica: Sigo.

Kast, V. (1993). Imagination as Space of Freedom: Dialogue Between the Ego and the Unconscious. New York: Fromm.

Signell, K. A. (1990) Wisdom of the Heart: Working with Women's Dreams. New York: Bantam.

Singer, J. (1994). Boundaries of the Soul. New York: Anchor Doubleday.

Weaver, R. (1973). The Old Wise Woman: A Study of Active Imagination. Boston: Shambhala.

Weinrib, E. (1983). Images of the Self: The Sandplay Therapy Process. Boston: Sigo

Maslow. "Religious Aspects of Peak-Experiences." (RA)

Maslow. "The 'Core-Religious' or 'Transcendent,' Experience." (CR)

Reiff, Philip. The Triumph of the Therapeutic. (TTT)

Wilber, Ken. "Psychologia Perennis: The Spectrum of Consciousness." (PP)

C.G.Jung, Psychology and Religion: West and East (Princeton, N.J: Princeton University Press, 1969). P.556

<u>Maslow recommended reading—Maslow's books</u>

Motivation and Personality, 3rd Ed. New York: Harper & Row, 1987

The Farther Reaches of Human: Penguin Books, 1976

Toward a Psychology of Being, 3rd Ed. New York: Wiley, 1998

Maslow on Management New York: Wiley, 1998

Religions, Values and Peak-Experiences Penguin, 1986

The Right to be Human, A Biography of Abraham Maslow. Edward Hoffman. McGraw-Hill, 1988

New Pathways in Psychology : Maslow & the Post-Freudian Revolution. Colin Wilson. New American Library, 1972

An Introduction to Theories of Personality. B.R. Hergenhan. Prentice Hall.

Best Maslow links

http://www/maslow.com/

http://www.mdani.demon.co.uk/archive/MDMaslow.htm

http://www.wynja.com/personality/maslow.html

http://www.connect.net/georgen/

http://funnelweb.utcc.utk.edu/~gwynne/default.html

http://www.ship.edu/~cgboeree/perscontents.html

http://members.aol.com/KatharenaE/private/Philo/Maslow/maslow.html

http://web.utk.edu/~gwynne/**maslow**.htm

http://www.deepermind.com/

http://honolulu.hawaii.edu/intranet/committees/FacDevCom/guidebk/teachtip/maslow.htm

http://www.businessballs.com/maslow.htm

http://www.dushkin.com/connectext/psy/ch09/ch09.mhtml

Other books and sources:

The Handbook of Jungian Psychology by Renos K. Parpadopoulos

Abraham Maslow, Toward a Psychology of Being, 1960

(Abraham Maslow, 1954 pp. 155-156.)

(Jung, 1969, b: 153). (The Psychology of the child archetype)

(Jung 1969 a: 38).

Institute for Management Excellence. (2001). The Nine Basic Human Needs. *Online Newsletter.* Retrieved February 2004, from http://www.itstime.com/print/jun97p.htm

James, W. (1892/1962). *Psychology: Briefer Course.* New York: Collier.

Maslow, A. (1943). A Theory of Human Motivation. *Psychological Review, 50,* 370-396. Retrieved June 2001, from http://psychclassics.yorku.ca/Maslow/motivation.htm.

Maslow, A. (1954). *Motivation and Personality.* New York: Harper.

Maslow, A. (1971). *The Farther Reaches of Human nature.* New York: The Viking Press.

Maslow, A., & Lowery, R. (Ed.). (1998). *Toward a Psychology of Being* (3rd ed.). New York: Wiley & Sons.

Mathes, E. (1981, Fall). Maslow's Hierarchy of Needs as a Guide for Living. *Journal of Humanistic Psychology, 21*, 69-72.

Nohria, N., Lawrence, P., & Wilson, E. (2001). *Driven: How Human Nature Shapes our Choices.* San Francisco: Jossey-Bass.

Norwood, G. (1999). Maslow's Hierarchy of Needs. *The Truth Vectors* (Part I). Retrieved May 2002, from http://www.deepermind.com/20maslow.htm

Ryan, R., & Deci, E. (2000). Self-determination theory and the Facilitation of Intrinsic Motivation, Social Development, and Well-being. *American Psychologist, 55*(1), 68-78. Retrieved February 2004, from http://www.psych.rochester.edu/SDT/publications/documents/2000RyanDeciSDT.pdf.

Soper, B., Milford, G., & Rosenthal, G. (1995). Belief When Evidence Does not Support Theory. *Psychology & Marketing, 12*(5), 415-422.

Thompson, M., Grace, C., & Cohen, L. (2001). *Best Friends, Worst Enemies: Understanding the Social Lives of Children.* New York: Ballantine Books. http://www.amazon.com/exec/obidos/ASIN/0345438094/qid=1024322725/sr=2-1/ref=sr_2_1/103-0382559-6049463

Wahba, A., & Bridgewell, L. (1976). Maslow Reconsidered: A Review of Research on the Need

Hierarchy Theory. *Organizational Behavior and Human Performance, 15*, 212-240.

Waitley, D. (1996). *The New Dynamics of Goal Setting: Flextactics for a Fast-changing World.* New York: William Morrow.

Third Force: The Psychology of Abraham Maslow. By Frank G. Goble

Mowrer, O. Hobart, "Symposium on Science; Society and the Public's Heath-Ethical Issues, "Johns Hopkins University, 1966.

Readings for those who want to go further than this book.

Maslow, Abraham H, *Motivation and Personality*, 2nd. ed., New York, Harper & Row, 1970 ISBN 0060419873

A. H. Maslow. *A Theory of Human Motivation.* Psychological Review, 50, 370-396. (1943)

A. H. Maslow. *Eupsyhceian Management.* (1965). Note that the Andy Kay featured in this book is the Andy Kay of Kaypro. Hardcover ISBN 0870940562, Paperback ISBN 025600353X

M. A. Wahba & L. G. Bridwell. *Maslow Reconsidered: A Review of Research on the Need Hierarchy Theory.* Organizational Behavior and Human Performance, 15, 212-240. (1976).

Bucke. "First Words"

Maslow. "Religious Aspects of Peak-Experiences."

Maslow. "The 'Core-Religious' or 'Transcendent,' Experience."

Reiff, Philip. The Triumph of the Therapeutic.

Wilber, Ken. "Psychologia Perennis: The Spectrum of Consciousness."

Maslow, A. 1968. Cognition of Being in the Peak-experiences. In: Toward a psychology of being. 2nd Ed. New York: Van Nostrand Reinhold Co. Chapter 6.

Maslow, A. H. 1970. Religions, Values, and Peak Experiences. New York: Viking Press.

Jung, C. G 1960. On the Nature of the Psyche. In: Read, H., and others, eds. The collected works of C.G.Jung (vol.8). New York: Pantheon.

Jung, C.G. 1964. Approaching the Unconscious. In: Jung, C.G., ed. Man and his Symbols. New York: Dell: 1-94

Authoritative Communities. The Scientific Case for Nurturing the Whole Child. by Cathleen Kovner Kline

Maslow, A. (1961). Toward a Psychology of Being. New York: Van Nostrand.

Maslow, A. (1964). Religions, Values, and Peak-experiences. New York: Viking.

Maslow, A. (1970). Motivation and Personality (2nd ed.). New York: Harper & Row.

Theoretical Models of Counseling and Psychotherapy by Kevin A. Fall, Janice Miner Holden, Andre Marquis

Psychology, Religion, and Spirituality by David Fontana

Jung, C. G. (1962). *Symbols of Transformation: An Analysis of the Prelude to a Case of Schizophrenia* (Vol. 2, R. F. C. Hull, Trans.). New York: Harper & Brothers.

Jung, C. G. (1989a). *Memories, Dreams, Reflections* (Rev. ed., C. Winston & R. Winston, Trans.) (A. Jaffe, Ed.). New York: Random House, Inc.

Jung, C. G. (1989b). *Psychology and Religion: West and East* (2nd ed., R. F. C. Hull, Trans.). Princeton, NJ: Princeton University Press.

Religion, Values, and Peak Experiences, Maslow, 1964

Book: Psychology, Religion, and Spirituality, by David Fontana

Other books by this author

Book 1:
Rumi & Self Psychology.   (Psychology of Tranquility)

Two astonishing perspectives for the discipline and science of self-transformation: Rumi's Poetic language vs. Carl Jung's psychological Language.

This book describes concepts like self respect, self liberation, self discipline, self assertion etc in a poetic and psychological language.

Book 2:
A Therapy Dialogue

A session-by-session therapy dialogue with an educated client who went through the self-actualization and self-growth processes. This book walks the reader through the process of therapy. In a step-by-step guide, it discusses what it means to live a life of "false self" and how to find a sense of "real self". It discusses a wide variety of issues like anxiety, family relationships, romantic relationships, negative behaviors and emotions and how to get rid of them, how to get to our full potential, what happiness really means, what is the difference between love and anxious attachment, what is assertiveness, how to process suppressed memories, and how to be able to see deeper into people's intentions, not just their behavior.

Book 3:
There is one religion:
The religion of KNOW THYSELF.

This book attempts to answer those seemingly ordinary questions of life with deep factual/practical answers. How do I get to my core being? Who am I? What do I do with my religion, culture, environment, family, gender, childhood etc., and how should I interact with these aspects of my identity? I feel like I have no use for some of these concepts. Do I need to learn about them, and if so, why? How do I put meaning to my life? What do I do with my emotional baggage? Others say I have it all, so why do I feel empty, sometimes? Why do I have such an emotional pain and can't cure it? I have so many people around me, so why do I feel lonely sometimes?

In this book there is a case example of an individual who learned about her culture, religion, and family background to ease her self-growth process. An individual who moved from East to West in her teen life, and used her immigration experience as a blessing, considering herself privileged to have had experienced living in two seemingly different countries in her lifetime..She came to learn that this experience had expanded her mind and thought in ways that would not have been possible if she had not immigrated. She also learned ways to learn and acknowledge the aspects of her life that she had escaped from, and found the experience fulfilling and uplifting. She felt a sense of having control over her life, picking what works, getting rid of whatever conditioning does not serve her, and choosing her own destiny.

Whatever we hold, we have to learn about and experience. Only after that we can make an informed decision about letting go of what does not work. If we let go of anything before learning and processing, we are getting ourselves into avoidance and repression rather than freedom. We can't ignore the rules and expect good results.

Book 4:
Where is my place in this world?

From egotistical to altruistic way of existence.

This book explains how to move above and beyond one's conditioning to get access to an unrepressed and infinite state of being where one can see that everything is inner connected and there is no separation. To get there one must increase her level of understanding and put her life to practice. The more one experiences life with awareness and knowledge, the closer she gets to her wholeness and that unlimited potential she beholds.

SKBF Publishing
Self Knowledge Base/Foundation Publishing

www.SKBFPublishing.com
Expanding your mind, widening your world, awakening your consciousness, and enhancing your life; one book at a time.

SKBF Publishing is a publishing company dedicated to providing educational information for enhancing lifestyles and helping to create a more productive world through more aware individuals. Our task is to help awareness overcome ignorance. Our publishing focus is on research-oriented and/or reliability contented books, including subjects related to education, parenting, self-improvement, psychology, spirituality, science, culture, finance, mental and physical health, and personal growth. We try to analyze each book carefully and to choose the books we feel have reliable and valid information based on available research or the credentials of the author. Our team of experts review every manuscript submitted to us for its practicality and content.

Our mission is to publish information that expands understanding and promotes learning, compassion, self-growth, and a healthy sense of self which leads to a healthier lifestyle. Our vision is to make a difference in people's lives by providing informative material that is reliable or research-oriented. SKBF Publishing is honored to have the helping hand of a number of scientist, educators, researchers, intellectuals, and scholars working together to review the books before approval for publishing with *SKBF*.

About the Author

Dr. Rohani Rad has a Doctorate in Clinical Psychology and a Masters e in Applied Psychology. She is a member of American Psychological Association (APA), Virginia Psychological Association, and Applied Psychological Association.

In addition, she is the founder of a not-for-profit foundation (www.SelfKnowledgeBase.com) with the sole task of bringing awareness to a wide variety of subjects ranging from root-oriented understanding of global peace to child abuse. This foundation aims to be a bridge of understanding between the East and the West by generating research-oriented material and awareness.

Dr. Rad is also a researcher, and is actively involved with a number of studies related to emotional wellbeing, children's mental health, and relationships, among others. These studies are performed in both the Eastern and the Western sides of the globe for a broader perspective of factual information.

Dr. Rad has written a number of recognized and up-to-the-point books about the subjects of self-discovery, self-growth, and self-awareness from a psychological perspective. You can find more information about the author and her books on her website at www.OnlineHealthClinic.com